STAR WARS
THE LAST JEDI
ROSE AND FINN'S SECRET MISSION

WRITTEN BY ELLA PATRICK
ART BY BRIAN ROOD

Printed in the United States of America
First Edition, December 2017
1 3 5 7 9 10 8 6 4 2
Library of Congress Control Number on file
FAC-029261-17305
ISBN 978-1-4847-0554-4

Visit the official *Star Wars* website at: www.starwars.com.

SUSTAINABLE FORESTRY INITIATIVE
Certified Sourcing
www.sfiprogram.org
SFI-01415

Disney
LUCASFILM PRESS

● LOS ANGELES · NEW YORK ●

FINN WOKE WITH A START.

He was in a makeshift medical bay on a Resistance ship, dressed in a strange bacta suit. Sirens were blaring, the ship rocked with a sudden boom, and **Resistance** troopers dashed by.

The evil **First Order** had arrived.

The Resistance was under **attack**.

Finn needed to find someone he knew. His memory was hazy from the battle on the First Order's Starkiller Base.

"Buddy!" Finn heard a familiar voice. It was Poe!

Finn was glad to see his friend, but he only had one question on his mind.

"Where's Rey?"

Poe explained that the leader of the Resistance, **General Leia Organa**, had asked Rey to find Leia's brother, **Luke Skywalker**, the last Jedi.

The Resistance had won the battle on the Starkiller Base, but the First Order had tracked them down. The Resistance needed Luke's help to defeat the First Order once and for all.

General Leia told Finn that they were on the run from the First Order in deep space. They had jumped to lightspeed, so the fleet was safe for the time being. The First Order couldn't track them through hyperspace—**or so they thought**. . . .

"Proximity alert!" **Admiral Ackbar** shouted.

Just then, a Mega-Destroyer and thirty Star Destroyers leapt out of hyperspace in front of them. Somehow the First Order had tracked the fleet. **The Resistance was in trouble!**

Poe ran to his X-wing. He had to do something to join the fight!

"Don't wait for me!" Poe called out to **BB-8**, who rolled on ahead of him at top speed.

"Jump in and fire her up!"

Suddenly, the First Order warrior Kylo Ren blasted the hangar bay from his TIE silencer! Poe's **X-wing** and the other Resistance ships exploded in a shower of sparks.

Poe and BB-8 were okay, but the fleet of smaller ships was **destroyed**.

"We need to get out of range of the Star Destroyers," urged Poe.

"Full engines ahead!" Leia added.

The Resistance was in real **danger**.

Finn didn't know what he should do.

BB-8 projected a **hologram** from when Rey had said good-bye to Finn, before she left to find Luke. Then Finn knew exactly what to do.

He would go find Rey and help her.

But a young Resistance technician named Rose stopped Finn from sneaking away in an escape pod.

Rose hated traitors. Her sister had given her life for the Resistance during an earlier battle with the First Order.

Rose zapped Finn using a small **electro-stun prod**. She would turn him in for desertion.

When Finn came to, he explained to Rose that the First Order had tracked the Resistance through hyperspace. But Rose knew a thing or two about the new technology, including that it could only track something from a **single source**. That meant only the main First Order ship was tracking them through hyperspace.

Maybe Finn and Rose could disable the **tracking device** on the main First Order ship so the Resistance could escape without being followed.

They ran their idea past Poe. It was risky, but Poe liked risky ideas.

They would just need a **codebreaker** to crack the First Order clearance codes to get on board.

Fortunately, their friend Maz Kanata knew a Master Codebreaker who could help them. He lived in the glamorous city of **Canto Bight** on Cantonica.

So **Finn** and **Rose** boarded a small Resistance
ship and left for Canto Bight.
But they weren't alone. . . .
BB-8 had stowed away on board!

When they arrived in Canto Bight, Finn was in awe of the **glitz and glamour** of the casino. He had been raised by the First Order as one of their stormtroopers and had never seen so much wealth or flash in all his life. Canto Bight seemed like paradise to him.

Rose just tried to keep Finn focused.

"Maz said this **Master Codebreaker** would have a red plom bloom on his lapel," she reminded Finn. "Let's find him and get out of here."

Meanwhile, one of the patrons had mistaken **BB-8** for a game machine. BB-8 happily accepted the alien's free credits.

While Finn and BB-8 were enjoying Canto Bight, **Rose** was not. She explained to Finn that the patrons of Canto Bight didn't care about the First Order or the Resistance. They didn't care about right or wrong. They only cared about **money**.

Finn started to understand. It all seemed so beautiful on the outside, but knowing that his friends were putting their lives in danger to save the galaxy while the people of Canto Bight looked the other way made him sick.

BB-8 rolled up to Finn and Rose **beeping** about a red plom bloom. It was the Master Codebreaker! He was at a table nearby.

This was it. Maz had told them that the Master Codebreaker would help the **Resistance**. All Finn and Rose needed to do was introduce themselves and they would be on their way.

Suddenly, Canto Bight police stepped in, blocking Finn and Rose from the Master Codebreaker.

The police had found a crashed ship on the beach and traced it back to Finn and Rose. **They had been caught!**

Finn and Rose were thrown into a **prison cell**.

Time was running out. The Resistance could outrun the First Order only for so long.

Just then, a scruffy man named **DJ** grunted awake in the corner of their cell.

DJ said he could bust them out of jail, crack the First Order **clearance codes**, and sneak them on board the First Order Star Destroyer.

Finn and Rose were doubtful, but they didn't really have any better options.

Meanwhile, **BB-8** had snuck into the jail to help his friends. The prison was heavily guarded, but BB-8 noticed that the guards were distracted by a game. **Getting past them would almost be too easy. . . .**

Back in the cell, DJ pressed a few buttons and smacked the heavy door, and the cell actually opened!

Finn and Rose were **shocked**.

It was as though he had done it a thousand times before.

Finn and Rose were one step closer to completing their mission. Thanks to DJ and BB-8, they would soon be on their way to disabling the First Order's tracking system, saving the Resistance, and maybe even freeing the galaxy. . . .